THINGS THAT MAKE A DAY THE BEST DAY:

1. Having breakfast in bed.
2. Taking a stroll on a sunny day.
3. Humming my favorite song.
4. Reading a book with _____
5. Finding
6. _____ he fridge.
7. Look

World m

For anyone having a bad day.

Text copyright © 2017 by Ruth Chan

Published by Roaring Brook Press

Roaring Brook Press is a division of Holtzbrinck Publishing Holdings Limited Partnership

175 Fifth Avenue, New York, New York 10010

mackids.com

Library of Congress Cataloging-in-Publication Data

Names: Chan, Ruth, 1980– author, illustrator.

Title: Georgie's best bad day / Ruth Chan.

Description: First edition. | New York : Roaring Brook Press, 2017. | Series:
   Georgie and friends | Summary: Georgie and his friends are all having a
   bad day, so the cat and his crew of animal buddies decide to do their
   favorite things to turn their day around.

Identifiers: LCCN 2016024230 | ISBN 9781626722705 (hardcover)

Subjects: | CYAC: Friendship—Fiction. | Animals—Fiction. | BISAC: JUVENILE
   FICTION / Animals / Cats. | JUVENILE FICTION / Social Issues / Friendship.
   | JUVENILE FICTION / Animals / General. | JUVENILE FICTION / Lifestyles /
   City & Town Life.

Classification: LCC PZ7.1.C477 Ge 2017 | DDC [E]—dc23

LC record available at https://lccn.loc.gov/2016024230

Our books may be purchased in bulk for promotional, educational,
or business use. Please contact your local bookseller or the Macmillan Corporate
and Premium Sales Department at (800) 221-7945 ext. 5442 or by e-mail at
MacmillanSpecialMarkets@macmillan.com.

First edition, 2017

Book design by Kristie Radwilowicz

Printed in China by Toppan Leefung Printing Ltd.,

Dongguan City, Guangdong Province

10 9 8 7 6 5 4 3 2 1

Georgie's BEST BAD DAY

Ruth Chan

ROARING BROOK PRESS

NEW YORK